The Conflict Resolution Library

Dealing with Insults

• Marianne Johnston •

The Rosen Publishing Group's
PowerKids Press
New York

Published in 1996 by The Rosen Publishing Group, Inc.
29 East 21st Street, New York, NY 10010

Photo Credits: Cover photo by Maria Moreno; p. 15 by Maria Moreno; all other photos by Thomas Mangieri.

First Edition

Johnston, Marianne.
      Dealing with insults / Marianne Johnston. — 1st ed.
            p.   cm. — (The conflict resolution library)
      Includes index.
      Summary: Explains why some people use words that hurt others, how one can avoid insulting others, and how to productively respond to insult.
      ISBN 0-8239-2328-2
      1. Verbal self-defense—Juvenile literature. 2. Invective—Juvenile literature. [1. Self-defense. 2. Invective.] I. Title. II. Series.
      BF637.V47J64   1996
      158'.2—dc20   95-50798
                                                                                           CIP
                                                                                           AC

Manufactured in the United States of America

Contents

What Are Insults?

Insults are words used to hurt other people. Have you ever said something mean to someone? Has someone ever said something that hurt your feelings?

People who insult others usually don't feel very good about themselves. They may be angry at the world, or they may not know how to talk about their feelings in a helpful way.

◀ When you insult someone, you hurt their feelings.

When You Insult Others

Maybe this has happened to you. Your brother turns off the TV just when your favorite show comes on. You yell, "Turn it back on, you stupid jerk!" That is an insult. Whether you mean them to or not, insults hurt other people. The worst part is that using insults doesn't tell the person what you really mean. What you really want is for your brother to leave the TV alone. What you've done is hurt his feelings.

Insulting someone doesn't solve the problem. ▶

When Others Insult You

When someone insults you, your first thought may be to insult him or her right back. That's exactly what the person wants you to do. He or she wants to make you angry. Don't do it.

Think about why the person is insulting you. Is he angry with you, or is he just being mean?

When you've figured that out, you can either talk about the problem with the person or leave him alone to cool off.

◀ Think about why someone is insulting you before you do anything else.

9

Self-Esteem

People who insult others don't feel good about themselves. They have low **self-esteem** (SELF-es-TEEM). They want to make others feel the same way.

A good way to deal with insults is to build up your own self-esteem. That means that you feel good about yourself.

If you believe in yourself, insults from other people don't hurt so much.

When you feel good about yourself, insults don't hurt as much. ▶

Brothers and Sisters

If you have a brother or sister, you may be used to giving and receiving insults. You may spend a lot of time together. You may start to **annoy** (a-NOY) each other. That's when insults can start to fly.

Instead of calling each other names or hurting each other's feelings, spend some time away from each other. When you've both calmed down, you can talk and work the problem out.

◀ Time with a brother or sister will be more fun if you can avoid trading insults.

13

Luz and Inez

Luz asked her sister, Inez, a question Inez couldn't answer. Luz became angry and called Inez "stupid." This hurt Inez's feelings. She and Luz didn't usually fight. Inez figured that Luz was having a bad day.

Later that day, Luz **apologized** (a-POL-o-jized) to Inez. She said she was **frustrated** (FRUS-tray-ted) with the question. Inez accepted her apology, and the insult was forgiven.

Take the time to apologize to a person if you've insulted her. You'll both feel better. ▶

Strangers and Bullies

When strangers or **bullies** (BUL-leez) insult you, they want you to insult them back. Bullies often have low self-esteem. They want you to feel as bad as they feel. They enjoy seeing others feel angry and hurt.

The best way to deal with bullies is to ignore them. They will realize that you are not going to give them what they want, and they will leave you alone.

◀ The best way to deal with an insult from a bully is to ignore it.

Insults from Friends

Insults are hardest to deal with when they come from friends. If a friend insults you, ask yourself if it happens often. If the answer is yes, think about what kind of friend you have. Good friends don't make a habit of insulting each other. If the answer is no, think about why your friend insulted you. Maybe your friend had a bad day. Chances are you can talk about it and work it out so that it doesn't happen again.

If a friend insults you a lot, she may not be a very good friend. ▶

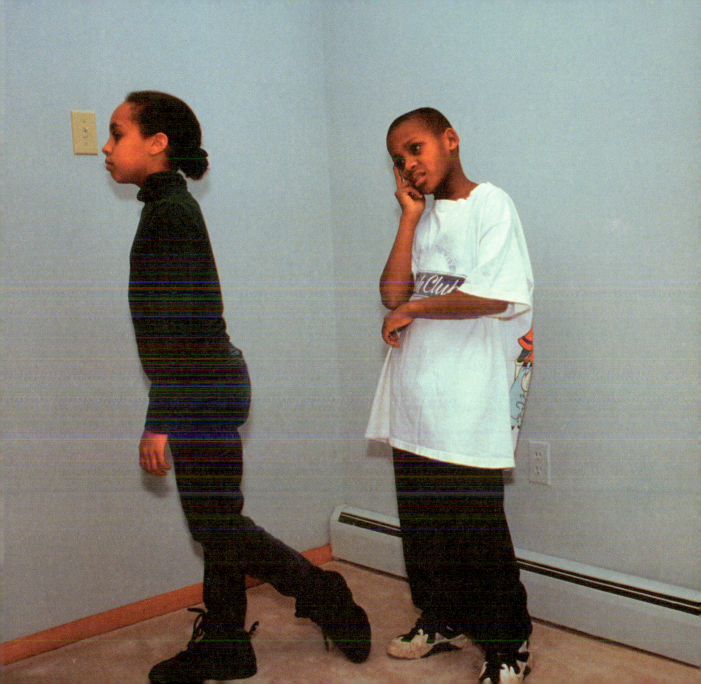

Alicia and Vicky

One day Alicia's best friend, Vicky, insisted on riding Alicia's new bike. No one but Alicia was allowed to ride that bike. Vicky said Alicia was selfish. Alicia got mad and insulted Vicky, calling her a spoiled brat. Vicky stomped inside.

The next day, the girls talked calmly without insulting each other. They both said they were sorry. Instead of riding bikes, they decided to play tag.

◀ Insults from a friend can hurt a lot.

Sticks and Stones

Do you know the saying, "Sticks and stones can break my bones, but names can never hurt me"? Keep this in mind when someone insults you.

Words hurt you only if you let them. If you really listen to the words of an insult, you will see how silly they are. The person who really has a problem is the one who insults others, not the person who is insulted.

Glossary

annoy (a-NOY) To disturb or bother a person.
apologize (a-POL-o-jize) To say, "I'm sorry."
bully (BUL-lee) Person who makes other people
  feel bad on purpose.
frustrated (FRUS-tray-ted) Feeling disappointment.
self-esteem (SELF-es-TEEM) What you think about
  yourself.

Index